Henry and Mudge
and the
Big Sleepover

The Twenty-Eighth Book of Their Adventures

by Cynthia Rylant
pictures by Suçie Stevenson

READY-TO-READ

SIMON & SCHUSTER BOOKS FOR YOUNG READERS
New York   London   Toronto   Sydney

SIMON & SCHUSTER BOOKS FOR YOUNG READERS

An imprint of Simon & Schuster Children's Publishing Division

1230 Avenue of the Americas, New York, New York 10020

SIMON & SCHUSTER BOOKS FOR YOUNG READERS is a trademark of Simon & Schuster, Inc.

READY-TO-READ is a registered trademark of Simon & Schuster, Inc.

Book design by Lucy Ruth Cummins

The text for this book is set in 18-point Goudy.

The illustrations are rendered in pen-and-ink and watercolor.

Manufactured in the United States of America

10 9 8 7 6 5 4 3 2 1

Library of Congress Cataloging-in-Publication Data

Rylant, Cynthia.

Henry and Mudge and the big sleepover : the twenty-eighth book of their
adventures / story by Cynthia Rylant ; pictures by Suçie Stevenson.

p. cm. — (The Henry and Mudge books)

Summary: Henry and his dog Mudge are invited to a sleepover in Patrick's attic,
where they watch monster movies, eat pizza, and enjoy a contest to determine
whose dog is the best popcorn catcher.

ISBN-13: 978-0-689-81171-5

ISBN-10: 0-689-81171-3

[1. Sleepovers—Fiction. 2. Dogs—Fiction.] I. Stevenson, Suçie, ill. II. Title.

PZ7.R982Heak 2006

[Fic]—dc21

98-020935

Contents

Raining Popcorn!

Henry and Henry's big dog, Mudge, were
playing outside one day when Henry got a
phone call. It was Henry's friend, Patrick.

"I'm having a sleepover Saturday night,"
said Patrick.
"Can you and Mudge come?"
Henry's mother said yes.

"We'll be there!" said Henry.

Patrick told Henry to bring a pillow,
a sleeping bag, and a flashlight.
"Cool!" said Henry.

"And don't forget Mudge," said Patrick.
Henry would never forget Mudge.

"We're going to a sleepover, Mudge,"
said Henry.
Mudge wagged.
"We'll stay up late," said Henry.
Mudge wagged again.

8

"And watch monster movies," Henry said.
Mudge wagged some more.

"And eat lots of popcorn," said Henry.
Mudge jumped up and did a little dance.
Next to crackers, popcorn was Mudge's
favorite food.
He liked to catch it in the air.

"It will be *raining* popcorn, Mudge!"
said Henry.
Flashlights, monster movies, and popcorn.
Henry could hardly wait for Saturday.

11

Bouncy

When Henry and Mudge got to Patrick's
house on Saturday, the living room was full of
boys and dogs.
Everyone was bouncy.

13

The boys were bouncy.

The dogs were bouncy.

Patrick's parents looked nervous.

They had a *million* knickknacks.

"Everybody to the attic!" said Patrick's father,
catching a knickknack in the air.

16

Henry and Mudge followed everybody
to the attic.

It was ENORMOUS!

"Wow!" said Henry.

"It's like a ship!"

The boys and dogs got bouncy again.
"Have fun!" said Patrick's father with
a big smile.

(There wasn't a knickknack in sight.)

He closed the door, and the sleepover began.

Giant Lizards

Patrick had lots of games for the boys to play.

There were board games and video games.

There were little baskets and little balls.

There was even a small bowling game.

23

But no one could play it because a bulldog
kept taking the pins.

When it got dark, Patrick's mother brought
pizza, and the monster movies began.

The boys and dogs ate pizza and watched
giant lizards eat entire towns.

"Mudge would be a good monster," said
one boy.
Henry shook his head.

"No," said Henry
"He'd just kiss everybody."
Mudge wagged and kissed the piece of pizza in
Henry's hand.

When the movies were over, the boys had a
popcorn contest for the dogs.
The dog who was the best popcorn catcher
would win.
Henry was sure Mudge would be the winner.

But he wasn't!
A poodle who did backflips to catch her
pieces won.

Henry didn't mind, though.
Mudge was still the only dog who could eat a
whole bowl of popcorn in one bite!

32

In the Bag

The boys played more games, then finally it
was sleeping bag time.

The boys got into their bags with their dogs.

(Mudge couldn't fit in Henry's bag, so he had
his own.)

34

The boys turned on their flashlights and made
silly shadows on the wall.
One boy made a kitty, and all of the dogs
barked and barked and barked.
The boys laughed forever.

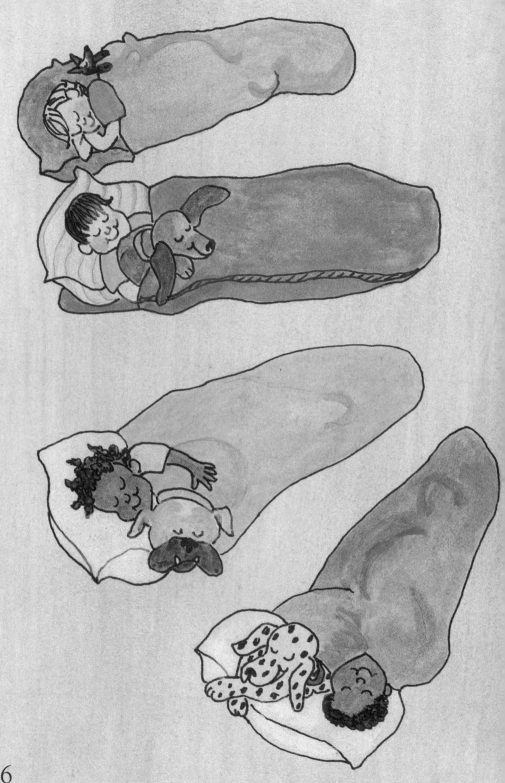

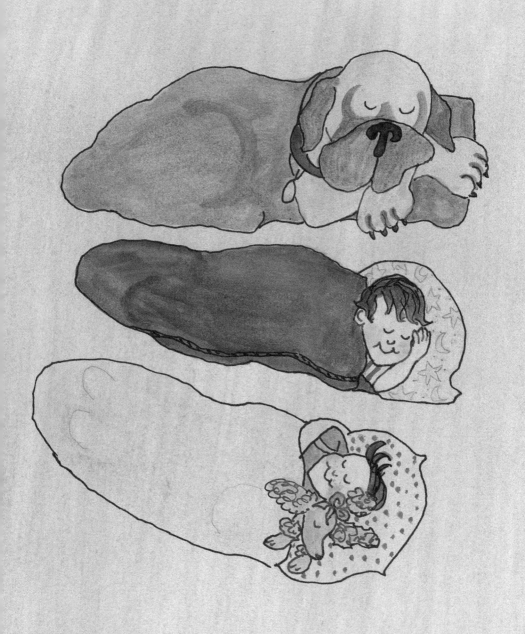

Then, somehow, the night finally grew quiet.
Everyone fell asleep.

Back home the next day, Henry told his parents about the sleepover.

"Mudge was the best dog there," said Henry.

"He was?" said Henry's mother.

"Yes," said Henry.

"Because in the morning, all the dogs were in
his sleeping bag!
And he didn't even mind!"

40